little bugs BIG FEELINGS

You Can Do It, Clover!

Hollie Hughes   Nila Aye

ORCHARD

This book belongs to . . .

_____

For Sam, Nathan and Charlotte
H.H.

To Jason for all his love and support,
thanks to you I also can
N.A.

ORCHARD BOOKS
First published in Great Britain in 2023
by Hodder & Stoughton
10 9 8 7 6 5 4 3 2 1

Text © Hollie Hughes, 2023
Illustrations © Nila Aye, 2023

A CIP catalogue record for this book
is available from the British Library.

HB ISBN 978 1 40836 718 6
PB ISBN 978 1 40836 719 3

Printed and bound in China

Orchard Books
An imprint of Hachette Children's Group
Part of Hodder & Stoughton
Carmelite House, 50 Victoria Embankment,
London EC4Y 0DZ

An Hachette UK Company
www.hachette.co.uk
www.hachettechildrens.co.uk

In the wild patch of the garden,
under brambles roaming free,
live little bugs whose feelings
are as **big** as **big can be**.

Come, step inside this story,
for the tale will lead the way,
to **Clover Caterpillar**,
who we'll meet out there today.

A happy caterpillar,
on the outside and within,
who wouldn't change a smidge about
the skin that she is in.

Little Clover's days are filled
with all she loves to do
and, in her life of joy and fun,
her worries are but few.

But caterpillars come upon
a time when they must sleep,
and awaken as a butterfly,
their childhood days complete . . .

LIFE CYCLE

1.
2.
3.
4.
5.

WILD FLOWERS

. . . ready to take flight and join
The Flutterby Parade,
where every flying bug shows off
the progress they have made.

Clover's scared of changing though –
she'd rather hide away,
and stay the way she's always been,
the way she is today.

"Come on," calls her friend Basil,
"you've not even tried it yet.
I'll take you butterflying –
it's the most fun you can get."

"But I'll miss cabbage," Clover says,
"and the burrows I love best.

And I don't think I could
balance on a flower
head to rest.

I'm so truly scared of flying,
and fluttering in the air,

and my Caterpillar Shuffle skills
might float away up there!"

"Don't fret," says Basil kindly,
"come with me to Queen Bee's Teas."
Then together they munch cabbage,
and sip nectar – freshly squeezed!

"Now climb aboard, and you will get
a butterfly's-eye view.
You can do it, Clover –
you can change, like I did too."

At first they take off slowly,
waving to their friends below,
but soon they're flying faster,
whooping loudly as they go.

WONKY WOOD

SUNBEAM STREAM

MINI MARKET

QUEEN BEE'S TEAS

MOTH MEADOW

CRAWLEY CROSSING

WOBBLY BRIDGE

LILY POND

FLY STREET

CRICKET GROUND

THISTLE STOP TOURS

HOPPY SLIDE PARK

HAPPY-TO-CHAT LOG

They visit Buddy Bee to help
fetch pollen from the flowers,
and race past Laurel Ladybird,
with acrobatic powers.

TOADSTOOL TOWERS

They glide onto a bluebell,
swaying gently in the breeze,
and Clover finds she's balancing
with unexpected ease.

Then Basil flies up high,
to his burrow in a tree,
and Clover cannot help admit
it's cosy as can be.

With one final step to take,
Basil boogies into line,
to prove he's still got moves –
it's Caterpillar Shuffle time!

Clover leads the dance,
followed closely by her friends.
Change, she starts to realise,
doesn't mean the party ends!

"Thank you, Basil," Clover yawns,
"you've helped me on my way.

Butterfly life might just be fun –
a new start from today."

Then she curls up tightly snug,
drifting dreamy deep asleep.

And, when she wakes . . .

... her wings have grown –

her change is now complete!

Clover finds it's not as scary
as she thought that it would be.

"Change is not so bad," she laughs,
"it's turned me into **ME**."

Then Clover flies with Basil,
in **The Flutterby Parade**,
as the other bugs all celebrate
the progress they have made.

And one thing that will never change,
or ever reach an end,
is the fun they each have found
in the other as a friend.

But it's time to say goodbye,
to the bug we've met today –
to **Clover BUTTERFLY**,
whose true story led the way.

We'll be back to visit soon, this
whole world beneath our feet,
and the **most amazing creatures**
we could ever wish to meet.